What to Do When You're Sent to Your Room

For Quin, who likes to be prepared
A. S.

For Farel Oz
S. G.

Text copyright © 2014 by Ann Stott
Illustrations copyright © 2014 by Stephen Gilpin

First edition 2014

Library of Congress Catalog Card Number 2013955677
ISBN 978-0-7636-6052-9

14 15 16 17 18 19 CCP 10 9 8 7 6 5 4 3 2 1

Printed in Shenzhen, Guangdong, China

This book was typeset in Cheltenham.
The illustrations were drawn by hand and colored digitally.

Candlewick Press
99 Dover Street
Somerville, Massachusetts 02144

visit us at www.candlewick.com

What to Do
When You're Sent
to Your Room

ANN STOTT

illustrated by STEPHEN GILPIN

CANDLEWICK PRESS

My name is Ben. I share a room with
my brother, my fish, and my hamster.

I hear the words "GO TO YOUR ROOM!" a lot, so when I get sent there for feeding the dog my dinner again, I know exactly what to do.

I know it might seem weird, but the first thing I do is write a letter saying how sorry I am and how it will never happen again. I've learned that it's best to get the apology out of the way. This usually helps to eliminate any further punishment, like having video games taken away.

I have plenty of snacks in my room if I get hungry. I keep a few packs of fruit gushies inside my Romeo Diaz bobblehead. My brother hasn't found them yet. Finding good hiding places for food is one of the first steps to being prepared for times like these.

My estimated release time depends on who sent me to my room. Mom usually lets me out early so she can put me to work doing chores around the house.

Dad can sometimes forget I'm up here. In that case, another note may need to be delivered.

But until release time comes around, I've got plenty to do—like sharpening all of my pencils, both ends, and starting to work on my birthday list. This is a good time to think hard about which new video game I want, Swamp Battle or Commando Force. Time alone in my room is great for this kind of tough decision-making.

A few weeks ago, I started a little redecorating project in my room. I've spent enough time in my room this month to finish wallpapering two of my bedroom walls. It looks awesome! I'm so glad my grandparents got me a subscription to *Sportz Today* for Christmas last year. My entire room should be completed by the summer. I should probably add tape to my birthday list.

If I need a break from redecorating, I introduce the cat to my fish and let my hamster out for a little exercise. Spending quality time with my animals is also a good use of my time. Animals can't order you around or tell you what to do.

Usually after dinner, my brother goes outside to play baseball in the backyard. I take this opportunity to make faces at him from my bedroom window. This is a great source of entertainment.

That reminds me: this is also a good time to sort my baseball cards. This will help me determine which cards I'll need to add to my birthday list.

Next, I organize my Screamy Babies collection. I'm sure there are a few missing ones that could be added to my birthday list, too.

After I get them lined up and sorted, I bury myself in them.
It's a great stress reliever. I think I have over a hundred.
I've been collecting them since I was four.

Room time is also a prime opportunity for improving my special-ops skills. I can usually count on my dog to help me practice some tactical maneuvers.

First, we have to dress for combat.

If I need ammo, I remove the heads from all my army men.

My pink stuffed bunny is the enemy.

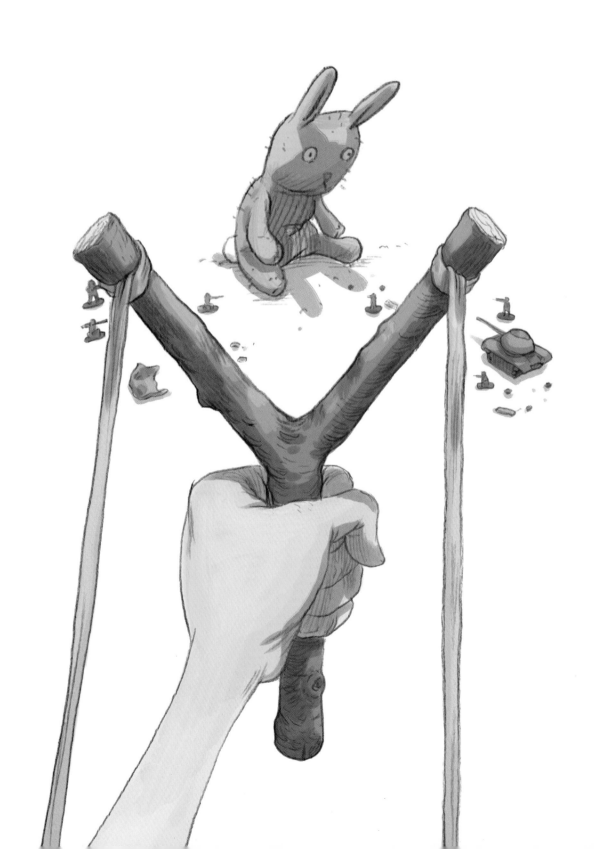

I know to always be ready for an early release.
I can usually count on my brother being sent
to his room not too long after me. And my mom
never leaves us alone together in our room.
She says she can't trust us.

I don't see why.

15